RAINBOW
magic
The Sporty Fairies

D1053976

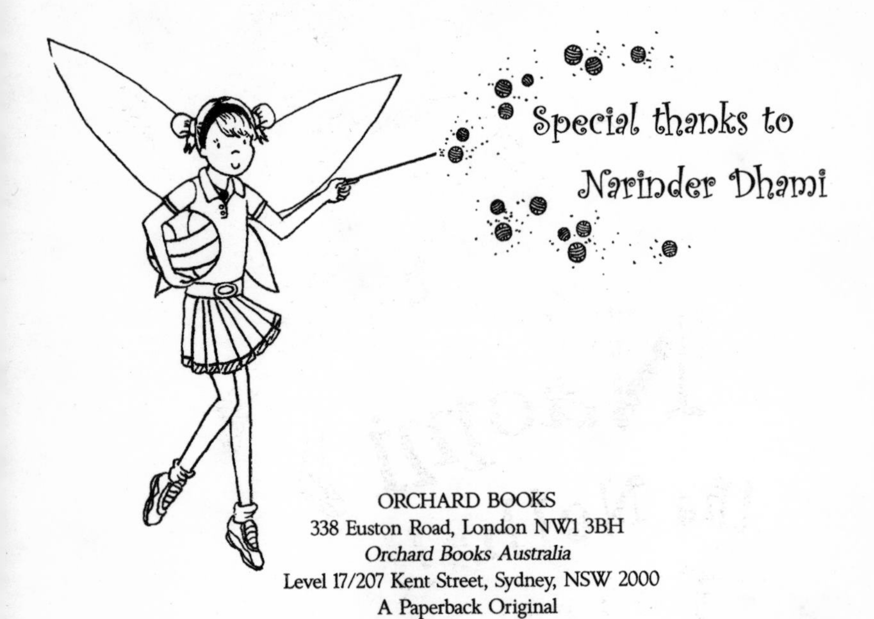

ORCHARD BOOKS
338 Euston Road, London NW1 3BH
Orchard Books Australia
Level 17/207 Kent Street, Sydney, NSW 2000
A Paperback Original

First published in 2008 by Orchard Books.

A CIP catalogue record for this book is available
from the British Library.

ISBN 978 1 84616 891 8
1 3 5 7 9 10 8 6 4 2

Printed in Great Britain

Orchard Books is a division of Hachette Children's Books,
an Hachette Livre UK company

www.orchardbooks.co.uk

Naomi the Netball Fairy

by Daisy Meadows

www.rainbowmagic.co.uk

The Fairyland Palace
Car Park
Coaches
Cooke Football Stadium
Riding Stables
Netball Courts
Tippington Town
Football Pitches
LEISURE CENTRE
Swimming Pool

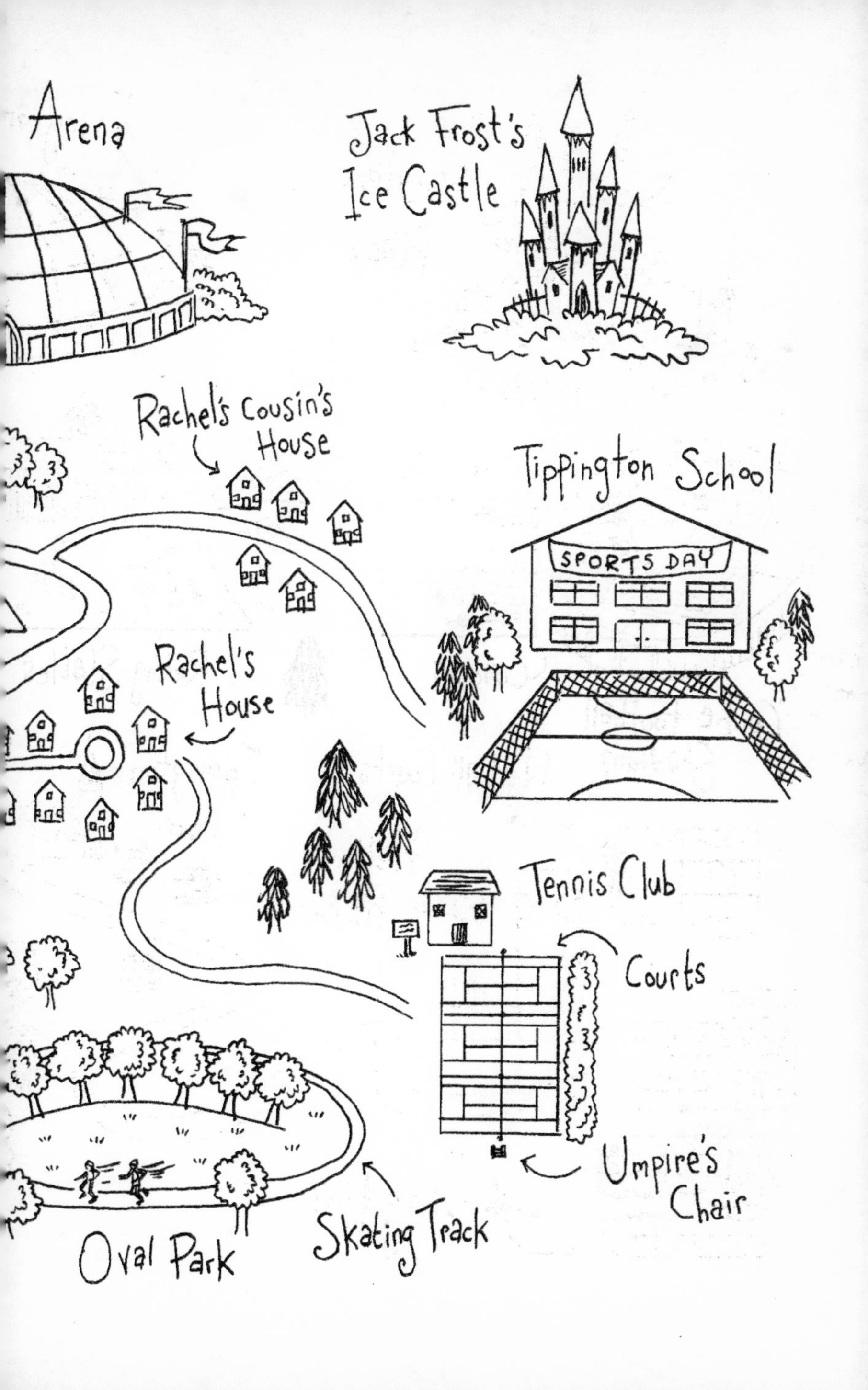
Arena
Jack Frost's
Ice Castle
Rachel's Cousin's
House
Tippington School
SPORTS DAY
Rachel's
House
Tennis Club
Courts
Umpire's
Chair
Oval Park
Skating Track

The Fairyland Olympics are about to start,
And my expert goblins are going to take part.
We will win this year, for I've got a cunning plan.
I'm sending my goblins to the arena in Fairyland.

The Magic Sporty Objects that make sports safe and fun,
Will be stolen by my goblins, to keep until we've won.
Sporty Fairies, prepare to lose and to watch us win.
Goblins, follow my commands, and let the games begin!

Contents

Spring into Sport

"What shall we do after lunch, Kirsty?" asked Rachel Walker, as she finished her apple.

Kirsty Tate, Rachel's best friend, grinned. "You know what I'd really like to do?" she replied. "I'd like to find Naomi the Netball Fairy's Magic Netball!"

Rachel and Kirsty shared a very special secret. While holidaying on Rainspell Island, the two girls had become friends with the fairies, and now Rachel and Kirsty always helped out whenever there was a problem in Fairyland.

"Remember what Queen Titania told us," Rachel reminded Kirsty. "We have to let the magic come to us."

"I know, but I'm feeling really impatient today," Kirsty replied. "If we don't find all the Magic Sporty Objects before I go home in a few days' time, Jack Frost and his goblins will win the Fairyland Olympics Cup!"

The Fairyland Olympics were due to take place at the end of the week, but mean Jack Frost had stolen the Sporty Fairies' seven Magic Sporty Objects. These magical objects made sure that sport was fun and exciting, as well as played fairly, in both the human world and Fairyland. But Jack Frost wanted his goblin servants to cheat their way to victory in the Fairyland Olympics, using the magic of the Sporty Objects to win every single event. He had sent the goblins into the human world to keep the magic objects hidden away and to practise their sports. But Rachel and Kirsty had promised the Sporty Fairies that they would try to get the seven objects back before the fairy games began.

Rachel sighed. "The missing objects mean that sports in our world are affected too," she added. "I wonder how many netball games are going wrong right now because Naomi's Magic Netball is missing!"

"Well, we've already found Helena's Hard Hat, Francesca's Football and Zoe's Lace," Kirsty pointed out.

Rachel nodded. "We can't let Jack Frost and his goblins win the cup by cheating," she said solemnly. "Especially as King Oberon told us that the cup is filled with good luck. Imagine all the mischief the goblins could cause with lots of luck to help them!"

Just then, Rachel's mum came into the kitchen. "Girls, have you finished your lunch?" Mrs Walker asked. "I don't know if you've decided what you want to do this afternoon, but I thought this might be fun." And she put a leaflet down on the table.

"'Spring into Sport!'" Rachel read aloud. "'On Tuesday, from 9.30 am, come and try a new sport at Tippington Leisure Centre – absolutely free!'"

Kirsty flipped the leaflet open. "Look!" she exclaimed. "Rounders, badminton, athletics, cricket and netball…" Kirsty glanced meaningfully at Rachel.

The Sporty Fairies had told the girls that any goblin who had one of the Magic Sporty Objects would be attracted to that sport, especially as the goblins wanted to practise their skills for the Fairyland Olympics. So Rachel and Kirsty knew it was possible that the goblin with the Magic Netball might turn up at the leisure centre.

"Why don't you go and try out a few sports?" Rachel's mum suggested, clearing away the plates.

"Good idea, Mum," said Rachel, jumping up from the table.

"It does sound like fun," Kirsty agreed.

The girls pulled on their trainers and headed into the village. The leisure centre was just behind the High Street.

There were football and cricket pitches in front of the building, and matches were taking place on all of them. There were also groups of people standing around, waiting to have a go.

"Looks like we're not the only ones who want to 'Spring into Sport!'" Kirsty said as they headed towards the glass doors. "Do you think the goblins might be here?"

Rachel nodded. "Maybe, but if they are, it's going to be difficult to spot them with so many people around."

The girls went inside the leisure centre and watched a badminton match. Then they peeked into the studio where a keep-fit class was taking place.

"Let's go and check out the netball courts," Rachel suggested, as they passed the gym. "They're outside, near the athletics track."

When the girls arrived, they found that matches were in progress on all the netball courts except for one. Two teams were limbering up next to the empty court, ready to start a game.

"Everything looks normal," Kirsty said quietly. "I can't see any goblins."

"Neither can I," Rachel agreed. Then she noticed a girl hurrying towards them. "Kirsty, that's my friend Abby, from school!" Rachel exclaimed. She waved at the girl as she rushed past. "Hey, Abby!"

Abby stopped, looking rather flustered. "Oh, hi, Rachel," she said. "Sorry, I was in such a rush, I didn't notice you there.

Is this your friend Kirsty?"

Rachel nodded.

"Hello, Abby," said Kirsty. "Is there something wrong? You look a bit worried."

"Oh, everything's going wrong today!" Abby replied, heaving a huge sigh. "I'm in a netball team with my friends, and we've just been challenged to a game by some boys who call themselves 'The Mean Green Netball Team'."

"The Mean Green Netball Team?" Rachel repeated. "What a name!"

"Yes, and they are mean!" Abby told her. "They've beaten all the other teams easily. They've even painted their hands with green paint and they're wearing green masks." She shook her head. "Talk about taking the team name too seriously!"

Kirsty felt a shiver of excitement run down her spine. She glanced at Rachel and could see that her friend was thinking exactly the same thing: could The Mean Green Netball Team be a group of goblins?

Rachel and Kirsty Join the Team

Abby bit her lip nervously. "The trouble is," she went on, "two of our players haven't turned up. The game is starting in a few minutes, and we haven't even got a full team! I was just on my way into the leisure centre to see if I could find some people to make up the numbers."

Rachel glanced at Kirsty again. We simply have to find out if the green players are goblins, Rachel thought. And this is our chance!

"Kirsty and I could play for your team," Rachel offered. "Couldn't we, Kirsty?"

Kirsty nodded as Abby's face lit up.

"Oh, would you?" Abby said, gratefully. "That would really help us out!"

"We're not wearing the right clothes, though," Kirsty said, glancing at the tracksuit bottoms she and Rachel had on.

"Don't worry about that," Abby told her, ushering the girls towards the court. "It's a taster session, not a proper match. Some of the players are wearing netball skirts and others are wearing tracksuits."

"OK," said Kirsty. "I'd better warn you, though, I'm not that great at netball."

Abby smiled. "Actually, nobody's playing very well today except The Mean Green Netball Team," she confessed. "Everyone seems to have butter fingers and two left feet, including me."

Rachel looked sympathetic. She and Kirsty both knew why everyone was being clumsy. It was because Naomi's Magic Netball was missing.

"We'll just have to do our best," Rachel declared in a determined voice, and Kirsty nodded.

"Well, I've seen you playing netball at school, Rachel, and I know you're good at shooting," Abby replied as they reached the court, "so you can be our secret weapon!"

Rachel blushed. "I'll try and get a couple of goals," she promised.

Abby found two bibs at the side of the court and handed them to Rachel and Kirsty. "Kirsty, you're in defence and Rachel, you're in attack," she explained as they ran onto the court. "Come and meet the rest of the team."

Abby took Rachel and Kirsty over to a small group of girls who were standing at one end of the court. They all looked rather nervous.

"Cheer up, everyone!" Abby exclaimed. "I've found two more players for us."

The rest of the team brightened up immediately.

"That's great!" said a tall girl with fair hair. "We're going to need a full team. The Mean Green Netball Team is really good!"

Rachel and Kirsty looked over at The Mean Green Netball Team, which was practising its ball skills at the other end of the court. The team

members wore baseball caps and were passing the ball swiftly and confidently to each other.

"They're definitely goblins, Kirsty," Rachel whispered, catching a glimpse of a pointy green nose under one of the caps.

"I know," Kirsty agreed quietly. "And look at that goblin spinning the netball on his finger over there."

Rachel stared at the goblin and gasped as she saw that the ball spinning on his finger was surrounded by a faint shimmer of purple sparkles. "It's Naomi's Magic Netball!" she exclaimed in a low voice.

"Yes! Now all we have to do is get it back," Kirsty pointed out.

"Let's get started," called the umpire, blowing her whistle. "We're playing for just fifteen minutes today." She flipped a coin in the air and turned to the biggest goblin, who was captain.

"Heads!" called the captain.

The umpire examined the coin.

"Heads it is," she announced. "The Mean Green Netball Team will start the game."

The goblins dashed quickly into their positions. The umpire blew her whistle and immediately the goblin in the centre flung the Magic Netball to the goblin on his right. Kirsty and another defender moved to block him, but the second goblin threw the ball high over their heads and straight towards one of the goblin shooters. The next moment, the ball was whizzing cleanly through the hoop.

"One-nil," called the umpire as the goblins whooped with glee and gave each other high-fives.

Kirsty glanced down the court at Rachel in dismay. The goblins were ahead, and none of their team had even touched the ball yet!

The game restarted, but once again the goblins were quickly in control.

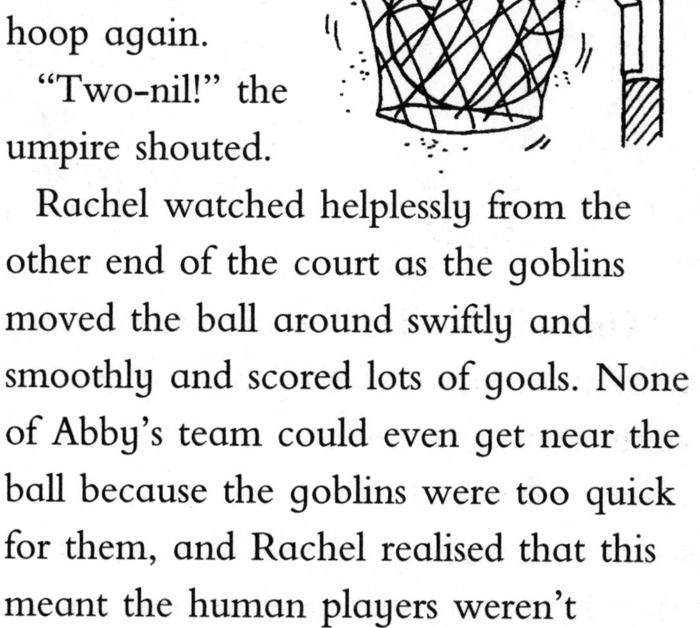

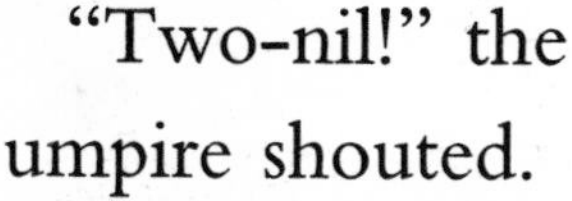

After a succession of brilliant passes, the goblin shooter sidestepped Kirsty and popped the ball through the hoop again.

"Two-nil!" the umpire shouted.

Rachel watched helplessly from the other end of the court as the goblins moved the ball around swiftly and smoothly and scored lots of goals. None of Abby's team could even get near the ball because the goblins were too quick for them, and Rachel realised that this meant the human players weren't benefiting from the magic of Naomi's netball. She looked across the court at Kirsty and shook her head sadly.

They were never going to get hold of the Magic Netball at this rate.

Then one of the goblins tried to lob the ball high up into the air towards one of his team-mates, but Abby jumped up and actually managed to intercept the ball.

"Abby!" Rachel shouted eagerly, waving her arms. "Over here!"

Abby flung the ball straight towards Rachel, but just as Rachel was about to catch it, a goblin leapt in front of her and batted the ball away.

"Oh, no!" Rachel sighed. She stood beneath the goal, watching sadly as the goblins swept the ball speedily down to the other end of the court. As she stood there, a shower of purple sparkles suddenly rained down around her. Rachel glanced up in surprise to see Naomi the Netball Fairy sitting on the rim of the hoop!

Naomi waved at Rachel and fluttered down to join her. She wore a blue and purple netball skirt and shirt, and matching trainers. Her blonde hair was neatly tied up with ribbons and a purple headband.

"Don't be sad, Rachel," Naomi whispered, landing lightly on Rachel's shoulder. "I'm sure we'll find another

way to get my netball back."

"I hope so," Rachel said eagerly. "It's great to see you, Naomi!"

Naomi grinned and slipped quickly into the pocket of Rachel's tracksuit bottoms.

At that moment, the umpire blew her whistle. "The Mean Green Netball Team win eleven-nil!" she announced.

The goblins cheered loudly. Meanwhile, Abby's team trudged away.

"What a whitewash!" Abby groaned, as she and Kirsty came over to Rachel. "We hardly touched the ball from start to finish. But thanks for taking part, you two.

We're going to try out some of the other sports now, would you like to come?"

"Thanks, but we thought we'd look around a bit more first," Rachel said. "We'll come and find you later."

As Abby waved goodbye, Rachel drew Kirsty to the side of the court, away from the celebrating goblins.

"Look who's here," Rachel whispered.

"Hello, Kirsty," called Naomi, fluttering out of Rachel's pocket.

"Oh, Naomi!" Kirsty exclaimed. "Thank goodness you're here. We really need your help to get the Magic Netball."

Naomi pointed her wand at the gleeful goblins. "We'd better stay close to them and wait for our chance to grab the ball," she suggested. "Look, they're leaving."

Two other teams had turned up to play a match, and the goblins were hurrying off the court, still chattering excitedly. Their captain led the way, carrying the Magic Netball.

Naomi ducked back into Rachel's pocket, and the girls followed the goblins, being careful to keep a little way behind so that they wouldn't be spotted.

"Right, we're going to practise shooting now," the captain said bossily, leading his team into the leisure centre. "We'll use one of the indoor courts where it's nice and quiet."

The other goblins groaned.

"That's boring!" one complained loudly. "Can't we do something else? We're great at shooting already!"

The captain glared at him. "What do you mean *boring*?" he snapped. "There's always room for improvement. Now, come on!"

He marched onto one of the indoor courts and the other goblins trailed after him, grumbling to each other.

Kirsty, Rachel and Naomi peeked through the open doors as the goblins began shooting at one of the hoops with the Magic Netball.

"They're scoring almost every time," Rachel whispered.

The goblins were now so confident that they began doing silly tricks. They tried turning their backs to the hoop and shooting over their shoulders or from between their legs. Sometimes they missed, but most of the time they still managed to score goal after goal.

Naomi sniffed as the ball whizzed through the hoop yet again. "It's my Magic Netball that's doing all the work," she said crossly. "Those goblins wouldn't be any good without it."

"Oh!" Kirsty gasped. "Naomi, you've given me an idea. I think I know how we can get your Magic Netball back!"

"What do we have to do, Kirsty?" Rachel asked.

"Naomi, can you magic up a new netball?" Kirsty asked. "One that sparkles as if it's magic?"

Naomi nodded. "Sure," she replied. "But it won't really have magical powers. It'll just be an ordinary netball."

"That's fine," Kirsty replied. "But can you also use your magic to make the goblins' hoop repel any netball that's thrown at it?"

This time Naomi frowned. "I can do that with a simple wave of my wand," she said slowly, "but the spell won't last for long because my Magic Netball is so powerful. Eventually it will overcome any repelling magic I put on the hoop."

"Well, my plan shouldn't take too long to put into action," said Kirsty. "We just need to convince the goblins that the real Magic Netball isn't working properly, and that we have a new, improved netball that's full of magic! Then they might do a swap."

Rachel looked puzzled. "But the goblins will only want our ball if they see us scoring lots of goals with it," she pointed out.

"Exactly," Kirsty agreed.

"But, how is that going to work?" Rachel asked, looking even more confused. "Naomi just said that the other netball won't really be magic at all. And the goblins will only believe it's magical if it lands in the hoop every time!"

Kirsty grinned at her. "That's where you come in, Rachel," she explained. "You'll have to use your brilliant shooting skills to persuade the goblins that we really do have a magic netball!"

Rachel gulped. "You mean I have to shoot and get the ball through the hoop every time?"

"That's the plan," Kirsty replied. "Do you think you can do it, Rachel?"

"I don't know." Rachel looked a little anxious. "I might not be very good at shooting today because the Magic Netball isn't in its proper place."

"But it is in the same room," Naomi said. "So some of its magic will help you."

"OK," Rachel agreed. "I'll just concentrate and try to score a goal each time the goblins are looking. It's difficult but it's not impossible."

"Go, Rachel!" Naomi said, twirling around with excitement. "And here's your new netball." She raised her wand and made a circle of pink sparkles in mid-air.

Then the sparkles transformed themselves into a netball which glittered slightly, just like the magic one. The ball floated towards Rachel, and she caught it neatly.

The goblins were taking turns to shoot at the hoop, but they had begun arguing about who was next.

"It's my go!" the smallest goblin screeched, trying to grab the ball from the captain.

"I'm in charge," the captain growled crossly. "I'll decide who's next!"

"I think it's time someone else had a turn at being captain," another goblin declared.

"No way!" the captain yelled.

As the goblins argued furiously, Naomi grinned at Rachel and Kirsty. "Now's my chance to put the repelling spell on the hoop while the goblins aren't looking," she whispered.

Naomi pointed her wand at the goblins' hoop and a rush of purple sparkles streamed through the air. Rachel and Kirsty watched as the sparkles surrounded the hoop and then quickly began to fade.

But, just then, a tall, thin goblin happened to glance up. "Hey!" he shouted, staring at the faint gleam around the hoop. "What's that? It looks like fairy magic."

Rachel, Kirsty and Naomi stared at each other in dismay. Had their plan failed already?

The goblins all stared up at the hoop, but the last few sparkles had already vanished.

"What are you talking about?" the captain snapped. "There's nothing there!"

"You're seeing things!" another goblin teased, and they all burst out laughing.

"But I did see some sparkles," the tall goblin insisted. He rushed forward and peered carefully up at the hoop, while the other goblins waited impatiently.

"OK, I can't see any fairies," the tall goblin mumbled sheepishly.

"Your shot," the captain ordered, thrusting the ball into the goblin's arms.

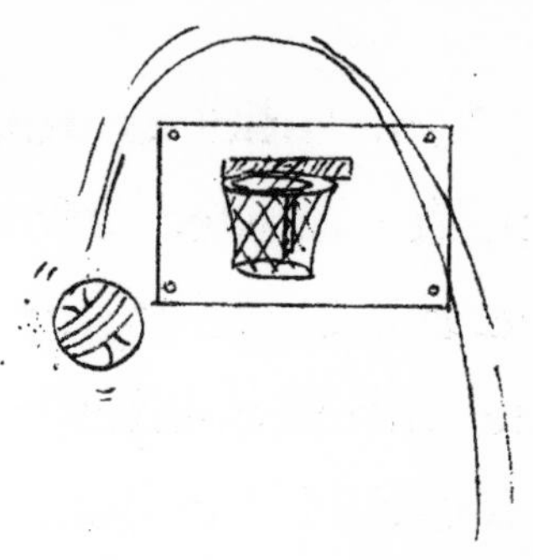

The goblin squinted at the hoop and then threw the Magic Netball towards it. The ball curved upwards in a perfect arc, but, as it fell downwards, it missed the hoop completely.

"What's happening?" the tall goblin squawked, looking confused as the ball fell to the ground.

"You're useless, that's what's happening!" another goblin said scornfully. He grabbed the netball and launched a shot himself. But again, although the ball whizzed straight towards the hoop, it missed at the last minute.

"The goblins are starting to look worried," Naomi whispered to the girls as the captain also tried a shot and failed. "I think it's time for you to do your bit, Rachel."

Rachel, Kirsty and Naomi came out from their hiding place behind the doors to the netball court. They hurried to the hoop at the free end of the court, the new netball tucked under Rachel's arm.

The goblins didn't notice them because they were arguing about why the Magic Netball didn't seem to be working properly.

"Here goes," Rachel murmured, positioning herself in front of the hoop and carefully taking a shot. The ball rose smoothly and fell cleanly through the hoop.

"Well done, Rachel!" Naomi and Kirsty cried, applauding loudly.

Feeling more confident, Rachel tried again. This time the ball caught the edge of the hoop slightly, but it still went in.

As Kirsty and Naomi cheered, Kirsty glanced over her shoulder. The goblins were staring at them from the other end of the court.

"The goblins aren't happy," Kirsty whispered.

Rachel grinned and immediately scored another perfect goal.

This was too much for the goblins

and they all came rushing over, one of them carrying Naomi's Magic Netball.

"How come you're scoring lots of goals and we're not?" the captain demanded.

"Oh, it's because I have this wonderful Magic Netball," Rachel replied, holding the ball up.

"But we have the Magic Netball!" one of the goblins said, looking puzzled.

Naomi peered at their netball. "Oh, you've got the old Magic Netball," she told the goblins dismissively. "This is the brand-new, super Magic Netball!"

Rachel took another shot. The goblins all muttered enviously to each other as once again the ball zoomed through the hoop.

"This new Magic Netball is better than the old one!" the captain declared.

"Yes, give us the new netball!" the goblins clamoured eagerly. One of them even began creeping towards Rachel.

Naomi frowned. "If you try to steal the Magic Netball, I'll turn Rachel and Kirsty into fairies and we'll all fly away," she told the sneaky goblin, lifting her wand. "Then you'll never get the new netball!"

The goblins looked at each other in dismay.

"Well, can we just have a go with the new Magic Netball?" the small goblin begged. "Please?"

Naomi looked thoughtful for a moment. "Well," the fairy said reluctantly, "we'll swap our new netball for your old one if you agree to leave here and go back to Goblin Grotto immediately."

"Done!" the goblin with the ball agreed eagerly, holding it out towards Rachel. But just as Rachel was about to take it...

"STOP!" the captain yelled in a very suspicious voice.

The goblin snatched the ball away from Rachel's grasp, and she glanced anxiously at Kirsty and Naomi. Had the captain guessed what was going on?

"Why do you want us to go back to Goblin Grotto?" the captain demanded.

"Because if you stay in the human world much longer, someone's going to realise you're goblins!" Naomi replied quickly.

"Your tracksuits and baseball caps aren't a very good disguise. And you know we can't allow humans to find out about Fairyland and Goblin Grotto."

The captain nodded thoughtfully. "That's true," he muttered. "OK, make the switch!"

The goblin held out Naomi's netball again, but, this time, before Rachel could take it, the captain sprang forward.

"STOP!" he shouted.

"Oh, make your mind up," the goblin grumbled, whisking the ball away from Rachel once more.

"We agree to the swap on one condition," the captain declared. He pointed at Kirsty. "She hasn't had a go at scoring. I want to make sure the new Magic Netball works on everyone, so let's see her score a goal!"

"Me?" Kirsty gulped. She'd never scored a netball goal in her life!

"You can do it, Kirsty," Rachel whispered encouragingly, handing her the ball.

Naomi fluttered over to Kirsty. "Take a deep breath and steady yourself," she told her quietly. "Focus on the hoop and make your shot as smooth as possible. And, most important of all, take your time."

Kirsty nodded, feeling very nervous. Her palms were sweating as she held the netball up and fixed her eyes on the hoop, trying to remember exactly how Rachel had scored all her wonderful goals.

After a moment, Kirsty made her shot. The ball flew through the air, and Rachel, Naomi and Kirsty all gasped as it touched the hoop and rattled around the rim. Would the ball fall inside or out?

A Glorious Goal

It seemed to take for ever, but, finally, the ball dropped through the hoop. Kirsty almost burst with relief as she grinned delightedly at Rachel and Naomi.

"OK, we definitely want that netball," the captain decided quickly.

Kirsty picked up the ball and

swapped with the goblin who had Naomi's Magic Netball. "Now, remember, you're going straight home to Goblin Grotto," Naomi reminded them.

"Yeah! We can show the new Magic Netball to Jack Frost," the goblin with the ball cried. "He's going to be very pleased with us!"

"Give the ball to me," the captain ordered.

"No!" the goblin retorted rudely, running off across the court. The other goblins chased after him, and Rachel, Kirsty and Naomi laughed.

"They're going to be disappointed when they find out that the new Magic Netball isn't actually magical at all," said Rachel.

"Oh, but it is!" Naomi replied with a wink. "We didn't lie. The new ball is magical because it's made of fairy magic. It just doesn't make people good at netball, that's all!" She grinned, flew over to Kirsty and took the Magic Netball. As Naomi touched it, the ball shrank to its Fairyland size.

Then Naomi touched the ball with her wand, making it glitter even more brightly for a moment.

"Thank you, girls," she cried. "Netball games everywhere will go well again, now, and I must return to Fairyland and tell the other Sporty Fairies the good news." She smiled at Rachel and Kirsty as she spun the Magic Netball around quickly on one finger. "Keep up the good work." And Naomi zoomed out of the door, leaving a trail of dazzling purple sparkles behind her.

"Well, you were right, Rachel," Kirsty said happily as they went in search of Abby and her friends. "The magic did come to us!"

"And now we're going to have fun trying out other sports," Rachel laughed. "And hopefully we'll have more exciting adventures with the Sporty Fairies, too!"

Rachel and Kirsty must now help

Samantha the Swimming Fairy

Jack Frost's naughty goblins have stolen Samantha's Magic Goggles, so nobody can swim properly! Can Rachel and Kirsty help Samantha to outwit the goblins and get the goggles back?

"Fetch, Buttons!" Rachel Walker called, throwing her dog's favourite ball down the garden.

Kirsty Tate, Rachel's best friend, who was staying with the Walkers for a week of the Easter holidays, smiled. "Buttons loves exercise, doesn't he?" she said, as Buttons bounded after the ball. "We're nearly as fit as him, after the sporty week we've had so far!"

Rachel grinned. Unknown to her parents, she and Kirsty had been on a new fairy adventure this week, helping the Sporty Fairies track down their missing Magic Sporty Objects. Rachel felt as if she and Kirsty were the luckiest girls in the world, being friends with the fairies.

"Good dog!" said Rachel's dad, coming out into the garden with Mrs Walker, as Buttons rushed back with the ball in his mouth. Buttons dropped the ball at Rachel's feet, then went to his water bowl to drink thirstily.

"Phew, it's hot," Mrs Walker said, fanning herself. "The perfect day for a swim, I'd say."

Rachel and Kirsty looked at one another excitedly. Swimming would be a great idea – especially as Samantha the Swimming Fairy's Magic Goggles were still missing.

"Ooh, yes, can we go swimming?" Rachel asked.

"Tippington Pool is closed," Mr Walker pointed out, "so you'd have to go to Aqua World in the next village." Then he frowned. "But the car's being serviced in the garage; I won't be able to drive you there."

"You could get the bus," Mrs Walker said. "The 41 goes all the way there. If you take your mobile, Rachel, you can let me know when you'll be back."

"Yay!" cheered Rachel and Kirsty together. They both dashed inside to pack their swimming things, then Rachel's mum walked them to the bus stop...

Read the rest of

Samantha the Swimming Fairy

to find out what magic happens next...

Win Rainbow Magic goodies!

In every book in the Rainbow Magic Sporty Fairies series (books 57-63) there is a hidden picture of a hoop with a secret letter in it. Find all seven letters and re-arrange them to make a special Sporty Fairies word, then send it to us. Each month we will put the entries into a draw and select one winner to receive a Rainbow Magic Sparkly T-shirt and Goody Bag!

Send your entry on a postcard to Rainbow Magic Sporty Fairies Competition, Orchard Books, 338 Euston Road, London NW1 3BH. Australian readers should write to Hachette Children's Books, Level 17/207 Kent Street, Sydney, NSW 2000. New Zealand readers should write to Rainbow Magic Competition, 4 Whetu Place, Mairangi Bay, Auckland, NZ. Don't forget to include your name and address. Only one entry per child. Final draw: 30th April 2009.

Good luck!

Look out for the Music Fairies!

POPPY
THE PIANO FAIRY
978-1-40830-033-6

ELLIE
THE GUITAR FAIRY
978-1-40830-030-5

FIONA
THE FLUTE FAIRY
978-1-40830-029-9

DANNI
THE DRUM FAIRY
978-1-40830-028-2

MAYA
THE HARP FAIRY
978-1-40830-031-2

VICTORIA
THE VIOLIN FAIRY
978-1-40830-027-5

SADIE
THE SAXOPHONE FAIRY
978-1-40830-032-9

Available September 2008